Chidi Only Likes Bl[ue]

An African Book of Colors

by Ifeoma Onyefulu

COBBLEHILL BOOKS / Dutton • New York

My name is Nneka. My little brother's name is Chidi. We often play together, and whenever we play the game Colors, Chidi says, "Nneka, my favorite color is blue. That is the best color in the whole world."

Then I ask, "Why do you always say blue?"

And he says, "Because the sky is blue, and my best shirt is blue."

"Perhaps Chidi does not know the names of any other colors," says Mother.

So, Chidi, here are the names of the other colors I know, and why I like them.

 I like red because Great-Uncle wears a special red cap. Only the chiefs chosen by our king or *igwe* are allowed to wear these caps. The chiefs are older and wiser than everyone else in the village and they help the igwe make important decisions.

Great-Uncle wears his red cap whenever he goes to ceremonies and meetings. Here he is, with two other chiefs.

 I like yellow because it is the color of *gari*. Gari is made from cassava roots, which are cleaned, grated, soaked and then fried in palm oil. Last of all, they are mixed with boiling water to be eaten with soup.

Here, the gari grains have been piled up in bowls to be sold by the roadside.

 Uncle John uses green leaves from palm trees to build roofs on houses. Here he is, making a shelter to store his yams away from the hot sunshine.

Mother's friend, Mrs. Okoli, uses green leaves from a plant called *akwukwo uma* to wrap up foods like *moi-moi* before they are cooked in the pot. Moi-moi is made from beans, and the leaves give it a delicious taste — though they look much darker when they are cooked.

Black is the color people in my village use to decorate their houses during the dry season. Usually men build the houses and women paint the walls black with *uli*. Uli is a juice made from the seeds of the uli tree.

The women's fingers move fast across the walls like spiders when they are painting, because they must finish before the uli dries up.

Some women make drawings, or add white spots with chalk.

White is the color of the chalks grown-ups use to make wishes for long life or for children. The chalk is cut out of the ground and then made into different shapes and sizes.

Here is chalk that Grandfather placed on the floor yesterday, when his friends came to see him. One of them, Chief Nduka, picked it up and drew lines on the floor.

"Chief Nduka has just made a wish," Grandfather said to me. "Women make wishes too, but in a different way. When a woman makes a wish, she picks up the chalk and rubs it on her belly. Wishes are prayers said silently."

I like pink. It is the color of the flowers that grow around our house. I always put some in my hair when we play Princes and Princesses.

 Cream is the color of the gourds that Grandmother uses. They grow on vines, and she cuts them in half, cleans them and stores palm-nut oils and soaps in them.

Cream also makes me think of the chewing sticks my sister Ebele uses to brush her teeth. The sticks are cleaned and cut into small pieces. When Ebele chews one, it softens until it is like a brush. Here she is, cleaning her teeth.

I like brown. Grandmother keeps two brown wooden stools in her kitchen. She sits on one while she is cooking, and I sit on the other when I am helping her.

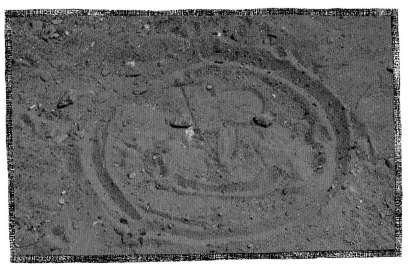

Brown is the color of the sand around our house. I like to draw pictures in it.

Here is a brown wooden board my friends use to play a game called *okwe*. The board has fourteen hollows carved into it, and the game is played with seeds.

Father is going to teach me to play okwe. He says it will help me count properly.

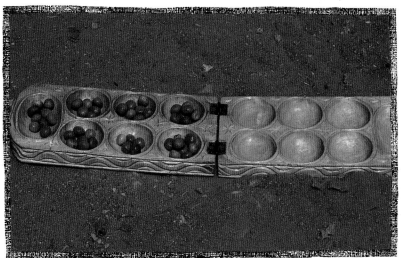

 I like the gold jewelry Mother wears on special occasions. It makes her look as pretty as the sunshine.

Mother has made me a beautiful dress of all the colors I like. She says I have been a good teacher to Chidi. But Chidi still likes blue best of all!

Textile design for endpapers by Chinye Onyefulu

First published in the United States 1997 by Cobblehill Books,
an affiliate of Dutton Children's Books, a division of
Penguin Books USA Inc., 375 Hudson Street, New York, New York 10014

Originally published in Great Britain 1997 by Frances Lincoln Limited, London

Cataloging-in-publication data is available from the Library of Congress

ISBN: 0-525-65243-4

Designed by Amelia Hoare   Set in Cochin

Printed in Hong Kong

First American Edition 10 9 8 7 6 5 4 3 2 1